CW00504954

38059 10115653 9

BARNSLEY LIBRARY SERVICE	
10115653	
Bertrams	19/11/2013
FAN	£6.99

From Wildthyme with Love

Proudly published by Snowbooks Ltd
Copyright © 2013 Paul Magrs
Paul Magrs asserts the moral right to be identified as the author of this work.
All rights reserved.
Snowbooks Ltd | www.snowbooks.com.
British Library Cataloguing in Publication Data. A catalogue record for this
book is available from the British Library.
ISBN13 9781909679139
First published November 2013
Other editions of this work
Ebook From Wildthyme with Love 9781909679221

Other books by Paul Magrs from Snowbooks:

Enter Wildthyme 9781907777059 (Paperback)
Enter Wildthyme 9781907777042 (Hardback)
Enter Wildthyme 9781907777462 (Digital download)

Wildthyme Beyond! 9781907777790 (Paperback)

Resurrection Engines 9781907777844 (Paperback) (short story)

Brenda and Effie Forever! 9781907777813 (Paperback)
Brenda and Effie Forever! 9781907777905 (Digital download)
Brenda and Effie Forever! 9781907777912 (Hardback)

1

Panda Lovey,

This is the last time I ever listen to you. Bloody hell!

'It's a Bring-a-Bottle party,' he says! 'Oh, I bet the place will be jumping by the time you get there!'

Thanks a lot, my furry little pal.

I ended up on a dead planet.

There I was, all glammed up, clutching my bag from the Offy, staggering through a mucky, petrified forest. I tripped over some horrid, dusty lizard thing.

Then I found the address you gave me. It looked a bit small on the outside, I thought, but I banged on all the bloody doors anyway. The lights were out and no one came to answer. You must have told me the wrong night, chuck. I was so brassed off I drank all the booze and left the empties lying around outside.

Next thing, I was quite pissed, but I bumped into a whole load of blond fellas who live in the woods together. They wear a shocking amount of blue eyeshadow and not a lot else. Anyway, we had a lovely time and later they helped me find my way back to the bus.

So – where did you say you were, lovey? And did you borrow my Time Scrunchy?

2

Iris dear,

I told you – didn't I? I hopped out in Paris, 1979. Rotten vintage, but who cares? I was feeling cooped up aboard the Number 22. Sorry my dear, but a little spell apart might be just the ticket.

Here I am outside our favourite bistro on the Left Bank. I've a glass of pastis and a splendid view of Notre Dame. And wouldn't you know it, but I've met a very classy lady who says she's in the art business. She claims to have pored over several of my critical articles..!

I'm popping over to her luxury apartment in the Marais this evening while her hubby's out. She tells me he's a proper Count.

Apparently he's out of town a lot, trying to be in too many places at once and she's feeling a bit neglected. Looks a bit like the top totty out of Space 1999!

Wish me luck, dearie!

Panda

X

Dearest Panda,

I set the coordinates for Paris but went a bit off kilter in the Maelstrom, that mysterious region in which Space and Time are completely buggered up.

Upshot is, I ended up here.

It's some kind of space city in the middle of a jungle of flesh-eating flaming plants.

LATER: Have found the bar. Full of space delegates. Some kind of conference, I think. Secret summit, according to the funny-looking fellas I've been sitting with. One in a jumpsuit covered in chocolate chip cookies. Another looks like a malevolent Christmas tree, but at least he got a round in, which is more than I can say for the Prime Minister of the Solar System.

They reckon they're here for a clandestine rendezvous with evil alien robots from another galaxy. They're such a tease!

You watch yourself with that Frenchy lady!

Xxx

Iris

4

Iris dear,

I did a bunk from the Countess. She had dreadful henchmen hanging round her pad. Plus, a roomful of knock-off art treasures and a very rudimentary time machine in the cellar. Seemed a rum set-up to me, so off I popped.

I'm in – of all places! – Putney. On the Common. Seems it's the 22nd Century and they're all going on about the Earth being invaded by something or other.

Anyway, you watch out who you're hanging around with. You shouldn't get involved in galactic politics and spies, you know. Remember what happened last time?

Must dash. There's a flying saucer landing on the Common! Looks like a bidet. We're going to lob some home-made bombs at it and defend our world against the alien fiends. Hurray for us!

Love,

Panda

Xx

5

Panda lovey,

Somehow I've gone and joined a dance troupe, something akin to Pan's People off Top of the Pops!

It all began when the bus was dragged down due to Magnetic Radiation into a graveyard for spaceships on a ghastly planet, all thunder and lightening. I met a welsh surgeon who lives with his hunchbacked boyfriend in a castle and there was some peculiar talk about his wanting somebody's head. Next thing, out came the Duty Free and I almost came a cropper in the front bedroom. I think he was one of those organ smugglers.

I escaped – a bit off my head – and I was found in the wilderness by Pan's People! Lovely girls who live in caves. Very given to the ritualistic worship of fire. They've got an elixir of eternal life and I must say, they do have the most marvelous complexions, but that might be all the make-up. Not sure what the sleeping arrangements are, but I'm game for anything. They've got some lovely moves.

Sacred Flame! Sacred Fire..!

Ta-ra, chuck!

6

Dearest Iris,

By the time you've tired of your Sapphic interlude (and do remember to bring some of that elixir for yours truly. I'm starting to feel my age. My ears have become quite flat.) I do wish you'd come and rescue me. Just when you get a mo.

Would you believe I'm still in London? I've been whizzed back to 1974 by your Time Scrunchy (I look ridiculous wearing it.) Somebody's playing silly buggers with Time Itself and causing dinosaurs to appear all over the capital. While I was stocking up on Seventies-style sweets in Woolworths I was witness to a stegosaurus trashing the place. He took out Rumbelow's TV showroom window next door, too. I almost choked on my Sherbet Dib-Dab.

Some fascist army general has tried to tell me it's all to do with the UK joining the Common Market, but that sounds rather outlandish to me. It's certainly put the tin hat on my reviewing anything for a while. No opera, no ballet. Covent Garden is just a wasteland of Jurassic faeces.

With love,

Panda

Xx

7

Panda, lovey,

I'd come to your rescue if I could, but the bus has gone haywire. Could it be to do with the cocktail shaker exploding all over the dashboard? I was mixing Martinis and steering through the Maelstrom with my feet. Bad move, I know – but I was celebrating. I'd thrown a little party aboard the Number 22.

I'd invited all my new friends from my latest adventure, which we had only just survived. More of those fellas in the blue eyeshadow and the blonde wigs! They were descendents of the ones I'd met earlier and they had fabulous legends about me, and the lovely boys delighted in filling me in.

We had a most exciting adventure together on a jungle planet. I wasn't quite clear on what was going on but we all had to put on purple fur coats and hide exploding red handbags in the trees. And then there was a disco beneath a volcano of ice..! It's been so dreadfully groovy, Panda, and ooh, you are being missed.

Much love,

8

Iris dear,

You've missed Christmas. I went off and spent it on a cruise liner. Turned out we were travelling through bloody space! I met a nice girl serving drinks who looked a bit like that one off 'Neighbours'. During the ensuing disaster (would you believe it?) she was instrumental in exposing the crazy saboteur. One minute she was dashing about in her maid's outfit, next thing she was making a noble sacrifice in a fork lift truck.

I wasn't quite sure what was going on at that point – something about angels chasing after us and I almost spilled my drink walking a tightrope over a bloody inferno – but somehow we narrowly missed crash landing on the Queen during her Christmas Day message. A quieter Christmas next year, please..?

Love,

Panda

Xx

9

Panda love,

Don't talk to me about Christmas.

I've just had one myself and spent it banged up in the slammer. A police station all Christmas Day, it was miserable. I was locked up with someone who looked like that girl off 'Upstairs Downstairs'. Bit severe.

I asked her, 'What are we doing here?' And she said, 'I don't know, but all I know is – they've junked this one.' I said, 'I beg your pardon?' And she said, 'Well, you can still listen to the soundtrack and look at some black and white snaps to see what's going on.'

I dug out some sherry from my carpet bag and next thing we were running about like it was a silent movie. I think I was in a tent with Rudy Valentino, and it was about then that I passed out.

I woke up later and they were handing out the sherry again and someone was doing a toast through the Fourth Wall, or so somebody muttered.

'Oh, is it open?' said I, and so I staggered through, finding my beautiful bus in the still-falling snow on the other side.

Anyhow, Merry Christmas, Panda lovey and let's hope

next year we find ourselves in the same Special Festive
Episode together.

   Love,

10

Dear Iris,

Honestly, I was only ever here for the train-spotting. New hobby. Thought I'd start at the beginning. Stephenson's Rocket was worth a gander. So here I am in Darlington, sometime in the nineteenth century.

All going well, until I come across this terrible time-travelling harpy in Shildon. Looks a bit like that one off 'Triangle' and 'Dynasty'. She's opened a gay bathhouse in a small mining village! What a to-do!

I say she's up to something nefarious, so I'm checking it out. Actually, she scrubs up rather well. Marvellous boobs.

LATER: Just as I thought. She's cloning dinosaurs and turning people into trees. Typical!

Love,

Panda

Xx

11

Dear Panda,

Here I am, freezing my whatsits off. We're conserving energy and keeping warm by huddling close together and rubbing each other vigorously every now and then. Haven't seen any penguins.

Turns out there was a second one of them space cabbages buried in the permafrost!

Stir-fry for tea.

LATER: Everyone feeling queasy after I cooked supper for them. I went back to look at the leftovers and that pak choi had gone a bit strange. Decided not to say anything.

Brrrr. Keeping my bed socks on.

LATER STILL. Someone's padding about in the night. I feel like a base under siege, I really do.

I hope no one starts mutating in the night. I can't bear it when that happens.

Love,

12

Iris dear,

On a mission for MIAOW. Visiting a Wildfowl Sanctuary of all places. Something about weather balloons and a missing professor. It all sounded very humdrum until – ZAAAAPP!

And here I am in the universe of anti-matter! Everything's the same, but the wrong way round. You'll never guess! There are two other Panda's here! One is much younger and far more frivolous than I, and the other seems to be terribly old and venerable. He didn't make it through the Event Horizon or whatever, and we can only see him on Skype, thank goodness. Looks like he might smell of wee, TBH.

We've met some absolutely raving queen dressed as a cross between Shirley Bassey and that fella off 'Star Wars'. I feel like I'm in a rather dodgy holiday resort. Everyone keeps saying we've been sucked through a black hole and goodness knows when we'll get back. I'm not even sure where I can post this card! Somewhere the sun don't shine, eh?

Love,

Panda xx

PS. Did anything happen with your Stir Fry of Doom..?

13

Dearest Panda,

Well chuck, while you've been languishing over the bloody rainbow, I've spent months in the caravan of Marco Polo! I think I'm in the old devil's harem..!

Don't get me wrong. There's been some spectacular scenery and I do appreciate the historical significance and all that. And some parts of the trip have whizzed by a bit faster because those particular episodes got junked back in the Sixties. Marco just shows off his snaps for those bits. They're a bit blurry.

But I think I've had enough of living in a caravan. It's pokey and draughty and bumpy. I've had enough of the chemical toilet, the Primus stove and the fold down bunk-beds. It's murder when we go racketing up the mountains and really, it is a bit of a bind being a sex slave *all* the time.

We've had some nice BBQs, I suppose.

Goodness knows when I'll see my bus again. I'm used to a very superior kind of mobile home, I realise.

Love,

14

Iris dear,

Investigating Neolithic stone circle (see pic on reverse) somewhere in southern England, circa 1978. V. spooky goings-on here with a couple of delightful old lesbians.

Almost came a copper at the edge of a cliff. Some devil dressed up pretending to be you jumped out and gave me a hefty shove. I had the screaming ab-dabs but managed to get a grip in time. Of course I knew it couldn't be you, gadding about elsewhere in the cosmos as you are. I suspect some occultish malpractice.

I'm being watched by crows. They're greedy for my black beady eyes, I think.

Apparently if you measure the stones' distance from each other and trace them through the centuries – they're actually moving.

In the very gradual, geological sense. In a very distinctive pattern.

Apparently it's the Hokey-Cokey.

Goodness..! The ladies are asking me back to their bungalow for hot sausage sandwiches! (Is this code, do you think?)

Love,

Panda

Panda Lovey,

When you said 'Neolithic Stones' I thought you'd met up with Jagger et al – again! But it was old lesbians and occultists – I should have guessed!

I've been in space hospital! A dreadful lurgy is rampaging about the solar system in the 30th century and I ended up with a dose. I met a nice Professor here in Holby Space City and his sweet robotic companion that he invented himself and guess what he's called?!

PAND – R!

The robot Panda!!

Such a friendly, helpful little soul.

Rather than nurse me back to health in the usual way, the Professor had a brainwave. We cloned ourselves, shrank ourselves down to the microscopic level and climbed into my ear hole to sort it all out. And so I've been on a Fantastic Journey through all my insides, Panda! You'll be glad to know I'm as glamorous and enigmatic on the inside as I am the outside! And right in the depths of my mind I met the source of the problem.

It was a giant prawn.

Probably it was a from a dodgy motorway services sandwich.

Food poisoning or ghastly alien intelligence?

You decide!

We sorted it anyway.

Hell of a job expelling our clones from my body. Best not get into it here, but put it this way - I'm now a thorough convert to colonics.

I was about to board the bus and zoom off into the ether when the Prof starts telling me he has a new post on Earth and they won't let him take PAND-R with him.

So – I don't know what you'll say about this, lovey – but I've got a brand new little chum travelling with me!

Love and hugs,

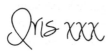

16

Iris Dear,

I am LIVID.

These people – are they something to do with you, dear? – intercepted the photonic-or-whatever-the-bloody-hell-it-is beam that my Time Scrunchy travels along and, next thing, I'm under arrest.

I was put on trial! Apparently for the crime of messing about with the course of galactic history.

'ARE YOU MAD?' I cried, but to no avail.

Everyone's wearing the most ridiculous headgear. It's a wonder they can hear a single word that's said. The judge looks a bit like the Mum off the 'Oxo' adverts, and she didn't look at all pleased when I pointed this out.

So there I was in the dock and they were going on about showing past episodes from my life! At first I was flattered and then I thought – oh, it'll be like doing a DVD commentary. I'm not hanging around for that. I had the guards escort me to the lav and, once alone, activated my Scrunchy and gave them the slip. Hurray for me!

Who are they to sit in judgment of me? Right now I'm on the run, it seems.

BTW: I will address this business of your ludicrous robot Panda next time.

Best wishes,

Panda Lovey,

Oh, but he's not a patch on you! Don't go getting jealous, my furry pal! He couldn't hold a candle to you. Mind, he does however mix a stonking Gin and Tonic and he never criticizes my outfits or my behaviour or anything. He sits calmly with all the star charts and picks out the nicest destinations for us to explore together.

V. sorry to hear about all your trials and tribulations and the fact you're on the run. They put me on trial once, for the exact same reason, and I had to watch all these old episodes on flat screen TV. And I was like, 'Hang on! I'm not even in this one! Oh, look at my hairdo! Who's that? What's this?! I don't remember any of this!'

Must sign off. Materialising now. PAND-R has suggested a marvellous place he's heard about. It's an actual living city filled with wonderful games and amusements! Perfect for a relaxing visit! He says it's called Sexxilon, or something. Sounds heavenly!

Ooh, the lights are fading!

Wish you were here!

MUCH love,

Iris xx

18

Dear Iris,

I have arrived in the middle of something I've been told is a Tim War.

It's rather like being stuck in a traffic jam on a Bank Holiday Monday. Absolutely everyone from all of time and space is here. People are chanting and singing awful songs.

It's all a bit common, frankly.

I went to fetch a cup of greasy tea from a small concession stand and the lady there said that this war is happening outside of time, at the level of meta-reality, and that's why nothing much is moving. She says, word is that the whole thing is going to be sealed off before long and no one will be allowed in or out, ever again. That seems a bit unfair.

I'd better find a way out, I suppose.

I haven't even met anyone called Tim yet. I wonder what he's supposed to have done to cause all this?

Best wishes,

Px

P.S I'd rather not hear anything about the fun you're reportedly having with your new robot assistant. TBH, he sounds rather common, too.

Panda lovey,

I hope you got out of that nasty temporal tailback.

It's no good getting irate over my new friend. As it happens, PAND-R is in my bad books just now. Our jaunt to the Living City of the Sexxilons was a bit of a bloody let-down. We had to do all of these daft games and tasks like it was management training. Then I got attacked by a frigging hoover attachment and all these mucky little skeleton men!

PAND-R is trying to make things up to me and we are en route to a mining planet where there are jewels lying around everywhere, free for the taking! He's promised me rubies and sapphires and emeralds. And we're going to be aboard a luxurious spa vessel staffed by handsome robots. Apparently they'll bend over backwards for you!

I could do with a break. I'm looking forward to what PAND-R calls a nice bit of chill-axing!

Love,

Iris xx

20

Dear Iris,

I'm relieved to inform you that I have returned to real, chronological time, courtesy of the Scrunchy. On my way back I met a man with a dove sitting on his head who kept trying to get me to go on some kind of celestial errand for him, but I wasn't having any of it. I said, thanks for the crème-de-menthe dearie, but no dice.

I'm in Scotland, and I'm staying in a rather nice B&B not far from Loch Ness. The landlord looks an awful lot like that fellow out of 'Crossroads.' Plays his pipes at all hours and tries to regale me with horrifying local legends.

LATER. I've had some lovely walks on the glens and down by the loch. But then I had a nasty turn when I was in the bushes. I saw something that looked suspiciously like a cybernetic plesiosaurus lolling about on the shingle. Oh god, I thought. Can't I get peace anywhere?

Then I heard all these horrible sucking and slurping noises. Naturally I drew closer to investigate.

Down on the shore I saw the local ghillie, the district nurse, the laird himself and my landlord. All four of them were gathered about the Loch Ness Monster – who was quite supine – and they all appeared to be… suckling at its doings. Teats.

I have never been so disgusted in all my life.

No porridge for me in the morning!

Actually, I'm going to check out pronto. I'm not staying in Scotland a moment longer, if this is the sort of thing they get up to.

Love,

Panda xx

PS. Just you keep an eye on that robot colleague of yours.

Dear Panda,

I came away with no precious jewels or loot at all and we barely escaped with our lives from that so-called luxury spa. All the flaming robots had gone crackers and were trying to massage and pummel everyone to death.

Not v. relaxing for your old Aunty Iris.

I went to the pub.

The pub was on a planet where they were testing everyone's intelligence through the medium of the pub quiz. PAND-R said I should have a go, being quite knowledgeable about the universe and everything. Well, our team came first.

Now I've been dragged into a subterranean sweatshop where clunky crystalline robots have got me working like a skivvy! In fact, all the geniuses from this planet are down here, in a kind of space-age call centre.

During our last fifteen minute break I took PAND-R aside. 'Erm, lovey… You're not just making it so that we only travel to worlds where robots do horrible things to humanoid beings, are you?'

And he looked so aggrieved! 'Iris!' he gasped. 'Why ever would you think such a thing?'

Hmmm.

Love,

22

Iris Dearest,

Somewhere ghastly. Just have a look at the picture on the other side of this. What a desolate, howling wilderness! Already I've had to flee from an Atrocious Snowman, several Synthetic Men and something lissom in a leotard who keeps adopting suggestive postures. On the plus side, I have also met several interesting women. Including five ladies who all claim to be five different versions of your own good self!

We've all been brought here by the mystical powers of some absolutely awful foe from the future who is using something called a pooper scooper or something to transport us here.

Five you's! Five buses! I've looked all over this lousy place, thinking I would find *YOU* you, but I haven't yet!

We've had to fight off the Voobi, the Gaar, the Bummies and the Chumbloids. As your very earliest incarnation cackled: 'Thank goodness only the most rubbish monsters got pooper-scoopered and brought here.'

LATER: We're in something v. like the ballroom inside Blackpool Tower for a final confrontation with our ultimate foe. And guess who the little fecker is, eh? Playing the organ and rising out of the floor?

PAND-R!!

I am REALLY NOT making this up!

Love,

Panda xx

23

Dear Panda,

Ooo-er, lovey. I could almost believe your last asseveration that PAND-R is an evil genius and that he was behind your most recent (and peculiar) escapade. I must say, I've found him rather temperamental since I confronted him about his possible nefariousnesses.

He's kicked over a few bits of furniture aboard the bus in a fit of pique and smashed up some of my precious nick-nacks.

I am very disturbed to hear about your adventure of 'The Five Irises.' It is most strange that I wasn't included. I wonder if they edited in some old footage of me? I would hate to be left out!

We've been stuck on this godawful island for days, surrounded by a sea of foaming acid. PAND-R was no help when I was set upon by men in rubber suits. I had to beat them off single-handed.

Then! It was like – I was being told I had to jet off to all these deadly destinations all over this planet, risking life and limb looking for five keys to something or other.

Well, bugger that for a game of soldiers. I've lost my keys a hundred times and no one's ever come to my rescue, have they?

Ooh, Panda lovey, I do feel lonely. I so wish you were here!

Love,

Iris xx

Iris Dearest,

Sorry to learn of recent shenanigans. I'd never say 'I told you so.'

I imagine you'll be cockahoop to know that your five past and future selves, plus sundry old friends, made short work of the schemes of PAND-R. (Tom says hello, BTW.)

Your mysterious superiors attempted once more to nab Yours Truly, this time with the intention of making me their Supreme Being! I gave them the slip by cadging a lift with an Iris who has a look of the young Jane Fonda about her.

It was like trying to escape from a bus depot. Much honking of horns and bellowing of Wildthymes as we all decamped.

So – I've hooked up with a different you! And, following a swift half in the nearest cocktail bar, we've embarked on our first adventure together. Promising so far – primitive tribes in a steamy jungle, invisible monsters marauding about and – best of all – a mountain range with a ten storey high bust of ME carved into it!

Love,

Panda xx

Panda lovey,

Sounds like you're having fun. Good for you.

I, meanwhile, am stuck with this artificially intelligent associate of dubious intent. He fixed the coordinates to bring us here – an ancient, deathly world where the Synthetic Men lie in their sarcophagi of ice, deep underground.

There's a mad glint in PAND-R's eyes.

I'm freezing my knockers off down here.

Love,

Iris xx

Iris Dear,

Next on our itinerary (following the affair of the God-Who-Thought-He-Was-Panda) we were hauled into another dimension by a being known as the Cosmic Puppet Master. We were embroiled in a variety of lethal, dreamlike scenarios. Then things became a whole lot more complicated when it was discovered that the Cosmic Puppet Master's property backed out onto another resident of interstitial non-space who styled himself the King of the Land of Fictional Spin-offs! Turns out where he ruled, all your favourite characters from tie-in novelizations came to life!

Then there was some argy-bargy - something to do with building extensions and planning permission from the Council. The metaphorical police had to be literally called out and we made our escape in the ensuing metafictional melee!

Love,

Panda xx

Dear Panda,

This time I wouldn't let the little bleeder take charge of our destination, and I answered an emergency call from Earth. We had been summoned by MIAOW, so that I could negotiate with an amorphous alien intelligence – a gestalt entity that took the form of a gigantic bin bag full of vomit – called Samantha.

PAND-R was mithering the whole time I was trying to sort out a potentially fatal (for planet Earth) situation. His grumbling kept spoiling my concentration.

Nice, I must say, to be reunited with my one-time travelling companion, that rather brusque Jenny. She was the one who always got the runs whenever we travelled through time, which was a hell of a drawback, as you can imagine. Nowadays she heads up the North East branch of MIAOW, which operates out of a secret base far beneath the indoor market in Darlington. Quite a swanky secret base.

I said, 'Hey Jenny – how do you fancy taking on a new operative? What about a robot bear?' And I pointed out PAND-R to her. She was delighted, and he was royally miffed. I whizzed off – relieved to have the little brute off my hands.

I need to find you, Panda! It's no good you knocking around with a future me! Surely that's against the Laws of Time and that?

Love,

Cris x

28

Dear Iris,

Well now my dear, I'm not so sure. In effect, since this delectably young Iris is a latterday version of yourself, then I believe we've already been reunited, haven't we? And she's very much easier to live with than you. You'll be pleased to hear that you mellow splendidly with age. You have a much improved dress-sense, great boobs and are generally much more fun all round.

Congrats on finally ditching that electrical incubus and I'm sorry if you're starting to feel lonely.

We are visiting an alternate-reality Earth and are currently investigating an alternate origin for the alt-Earth Synthetic Men. We're having an alternate adventure to do with Double Agents and Body Horror and it's all very thrilling. Rather more gritty and up-to-date than I'm used to, actually. Better special effects too. This Iris carries a bloody big gun and I might just get one of my own.

Regards,

Panda x

Oh, do not forsake me! This wanton gun-toting, big-boobed hussy can't truly be me! You must have been hood-winked, my hirsute pal! And what are you doing anyway, sticking your paws into alternate timelines?

I was so miserable I got completely trollied and managed to materialize inside someone's television set.

Took me ages to realise what was going on. I had to round up all the little people who were stuck inside – the newsreaders, weather girls, continuity announcers, footballers, soap stars, game show hosts, game show contestants, detectives and serial killers and we had to climb through all the valves and circuits till we could get out the back of the set.

Found ourselves returning to full size in a TV showroom somewhere in London, circa 1974!

Just in time to see a flaming great Stegosaurus smashing through the window with his armour-plated tail! Gave me quite a turn!

Love,

30

Dear Iris,

We are having a rather butch adventure in space. We're on board a space ship and it's very oily and dirty. The captain's a lady, with greasy blonde hair (looks a bit like that one off 'Eastenders'), a big gun and a mucky vest top. Quite gruff. The whole ship is falling into the sun. It's a race against time, apparently.

That's it for news.

V v excited.

Love,

Panda x

Dearest P,

I've joined a cult. The rest are all fellas. We do lots of chanting and meditation.

The nice young tea boy (quite fit) has pointed out a number of items dotted around this country house which he finds suspicious. He pushed me into the broom cupboard to enumerate them to me:

A glowing human skull in our leader's study.

An Egyptian sarcophagus in the drawing room. If you stand too closely it starts flashing and making a funny noise. Turns into a time tunnel thingy.

Giant spider in the bathroom, which talks like a lady.

A roomful of mirrors which, if you touch them, can give you a nasty static shock and whizz you back to the Victorian Era.

That man who played the teacher in a wig on 'Grange Hill'.

I've told the fit young man that I find absolutely none of these things suspicious and I'd appreciate it if he left me to my soul-searching.

Love,

 x

Dear Iris,

Thinking about it – isn't it quite odd, this? My continuing to send you post cards back into the past? The you I'm with today – here in Versailles – doesn't have a clue that I'm writing this. She's off horse-riding and jumping through mirrors, doing battle with clockwork fops and having a dalliance with a pert young miss in a big frock. I wonder why I'm keeping this correspondence a secret from her?

While she / you were out I snuck back to the courtyard where the Number 22 is parked and I crept up to the top deck where all her / your personal things are stowed away. I hunted through private drawers and found diaries and a cardboard box filled with postcards from all over Space and Time – all of them centuries-old. I found this very one – which is why it's so tatty and frayed.

There are about ten cards left after this. I wonder what happens? Has she lost the rest? Do I stop writing to you?

My poor addled head. I feel quite philosophical and sleepy. Being in France always does that to me. Must nap. We're having a ball later tonight.

Love

Panda x

Panda Lovey,

Your temporal shenanigans are doing my head in! Just don't you dare stop writing to me – and I think it's about time you got your fuzzy little self back here by my side where you belong. Capisce?

I'm in Blackpool again – supposedly opening an Exhibition on the Prom in my honour, celebrating hundreds of years of my adventures in Space and Time. But I think that might have been a trap. It's the mid-1980s and the Cosmic Puppet Master is up to various kinds of naughtiness to do with real living Space Invaders lurking inside an amusement arcade!

But I don't think I even have the heart to finish this adventure. I might just pop it on hiatus and go off to play bingo at the Pleasure Beach. I've not played Housey-Housey in years! Eyes down, lovey!

Yours Ever,

Iris xx

34

Iris Dear,

Your future counterpart can be rather brutal, I have to say.

We're embroiled in something not very pleasant to do with your future timeline, that strange 'Tim War' I almost got trapped in, *and* the fate of your mysterious superiors.

I have a strong suspicion that your future self has blown the buggers up.

Love,

Panda x

Panda lovey,

I've checked myself into a kind of Space-Age Butlins.
I'm here to relax. No, I'm not interested in volleyball or
learning to tango. And no, I don't want to hear about the
apocalyptic things you believe you've witnessed either.
I just want to sit at the Polynesian bar on a bamboo stool
drinking cocktails out of a coconut and giving the German
barman the glad-eye. He tells me it's Grab-a-Granny night.

LATER. Turns out the whole camp is overrun with
crabs.

Xxx S

Iris Dearest,

How funny! How synchronous!

I'm in the year 5 Billion ('What?!' you say. 'I know! Ridiculous! How did her suspension manage it?') We're on some ghastly far-flung Earth colony that looks suspiciously like the M25. Visiting an elderly pal of your future self, who's just one huge head in a bucket. He used to be an omnisexual travel agent called Mr Derek?

Anyhow – he was popping his clogs just as we arrived. Saved his last living breath to impart to us four final words of wisdom: 'Watch out for crabs.'

Panda xx

Panda lovey,

Still trying to find myself. (So are you, but I mean in a spiritual fashion.)

I'm in a Welsh hippy commune, getting back to nature with a sexy Prof. Up to my eyes in lentil bake and stuffed mushrooms. Drinking a lot of elderberry wine. Might stick around till the end of the Seventies. See how it goes.

Thinking of getting first dibs on the branding. 'The Iris Wildthyme Vegetarian Sausage.' What do you think?

Got told off for making mushroom vodka in the bath. It went a bit maggoty.

Love,

Iris. Xx

Iris Dear,

At a country house party in the 1930s. Telling Ngaio
Marsh that I love her murder mysteries. Going overboard
as usual and informing her I'm from the far future and
inferring that she will turn out to be the bestselling author
of all time. She is absolutely cockahoop. I compounded my
shame by claiming never to have heard of Agatha Christie.

Luckily, several brutal murders have distracted every-
body.

LATER: A giant wasp!

Love,

Panda x

Panda lovey,

MIAOW business once more. I've inveigled myself into a cabal of evil government scientists who have been working on a super serum. It apparently makes things grow to a hundred times their previous size!

And I've uncovered the wicked genius behind it all. PAND-R!

I know! The little monkey!

LATER. He's tipped a whole bucket of the super serum over himself. Now the size of a house. I'm writing this from an awkward position, clutched in one of his metal hands and wriggling like Fay Wray. Please excuse handwriting.

LATER STILL. Spent some quality time with PAND-R. Starting to think he's been misunderstood. Feel slightly responsible for bringing him back in time from his native 30th Century. Here we are clinging to the side of Big Ben. He's quite nice, really. Hoping to talk him down.

Love,

Iris xx

Dear Iris,

DIRTY cavemen. Ugh.

X

Panda.

Dearest Panda,

Do you ever wonder if you think about things too much? I mean, here I am, in the dim and distant past. I suppose we'd call it the Dark Ages. Jousting. Carousing. Banqueting. Lopping off people's heads. All that Philippa Gregory stuff.

So I'm whooping it up in a draughty castle and I'm wondering – what kind of an adventure is this? Would I call this a Pure Historical? Because I can't see any sci-fi elements, apart from myself, of course, and I'm not sure I count.

Could it be a Celebrity Historical? I mean, is King John still well-known enough to qualify? I'm not sure he is, really.

Ooh, lovey. I've drank enough mead to last me a flaming lifetime.

All in all I was quite relieved when the monarch turned out to be a cyborg from the future, heavily disguised. One of those future-fellas-visit-the-Middle-Ages-and-muck-about-with-stuff affairs.

At least now I know I've been in a Pseudo-Historical. So that's very satisfying to know.

Love,

Iris xx

Iris Dear,

Another overtly florid jungle world. There's no metal on this one so everyone is scavenging about. Of course, I was a prime target since I was lugging about a lovely canteen of cutlery I'd picked up in the John Lewis's sale. Next thing, a gang of ne'er-do-wells have shoved me down an *actual* well. And I'm being menaced – horribly – by a monstrously large, hairy green ball bag.

I am not making this up.

Anyhow, that isn't the point. What I want to tell you is that I have met an old gaffer who smells of widdle (and who looks a lot like TV's 'Catweazle') and he claims to be an ardent fan not just of you, but the pair of us! (And *not* your future self either because, he says, her novelty's rubbed off.)

You won't like this bit, I'm sure, but he says that you have become a multi-platform franchise and even he as a super-fan hardly knows what is canonical anymore! He says your timeline is more or less completely buggered up!

LATER. I've had to spend several mortifying days negotiating with an over-sized scrotum.

All love,

Panda xx

Dear Panda,

Strange little enclave universe. A junkyard in time. Bit pissed and confused, I must admit, but I appear to have encountered the very spirit of the Number 22 itself! I was expecting something a bit more ethereal than a miserable bloke with a Hitler tash and a dirty mac. I fondly imagined some spooky woman telling me how she decided all those centuries ago to run away with me, and how she was more than half to blame for our endless flight through the Maelstrom, that mysterious region in Space and Time where etc, etc. But instead it's like being confronted by Blakey off 'On the Buses.'

BTW, I don't know what you mean about my multi-platform non-canonical doings. Perhaps you mean my range of Spin-Off Audio Adventures, Original Novelisations, Computer Games and Comic Strips? Did I never tell you about those things, lovey? Not that it matters, of course. In the great scheme of things, I suspect that they don't really count.

Love,

Iris x

Dearest Iris,

I have a sense of foreboding – or is it foreshadowing?

Everywhere we've been recently in Space and Time, we have had glimpses of the same few enigmatic words. Overheard in a bar, on road signs, on somebody's t-shirt, on billboards, in poems and film posters. We have both remarked on the way this short phrase has been seemingly strewn through Time and Space, trying to snag our attention:

TIME GENTLEMEN, PLEASE.

It never fails to send a shudder through our vitals, with each and every iteration.

What can it mean?

Who *are* the mysterious Time Gentlemen, and why should we plead with them?

Ooh, isn't it just like an intimation of mortality? I said as much to T S Eliot, when we bumped into him as he left his offices at Faber and Faber. We were on the trail of disembodied aliens who were looking to take over the minds and forms of the Faber Twentieth Century Poets. I have absolutely no idea why they thought this was a good idea. They tried to explain themselves, but it all came out in gibberish, gobbledegook and cryptic blank verse.

I've noticed that your future self has become quite given to looking up at the starry skies and saying things like, 'It's coming!' and 'So it begins!'

I asked her, 'What's coming? What's beginning?'
But she just shivers and won't reply.
T S Eliot was no bloody help, either.
Love,

Panda x

45

Dear Iris,

Further to my last. A perplexing encounter. Met a blue bloke who was just a head in a box. He goaded your future self into quite a tizzy. Telling her that soon she'll face 'The Penultimate Question.' It was a very end-of-episodey kind of thing – the sort that you don't expect to see followed up any time soon, if it all – and we were out of there in a flash. Still, it's had me thinking – what *is* The Penultimate Question, do you think, lovey?

Xxx

P

Far as I'm concerned, The Penultimate Question is always 'Where's the bar?' and I can top that by telling you the *Ultimate* Flaming Question is always: 'What's yours, lovey?'

I think you should stop hanging around with her. She's making you all gloomy and introspective. I can't say I'm looking forward to one day turning into her. She might have a nicer figure but she sounds a proper moaner.

Here I am at the Earth's Core! I've met a whole bunch of reptile people who feel they've been robbed of their planet by the Ape Primitives. Well, they've got a point, I think.

And I've met a lovely dashing old gentleman, too. Has a look of Peter Cushing about him.

Anyhoo. MIAOW seem intent on genocide, so I'd best get that prevented ASAP. So I'll sign off here. Mind you tell that latterday me to buck her ideas up!

Love,

Dear Iris,

Your future self and I have had a row.

I simply said that if we're travelling about in time, then perhaps we have a responsibility to put right some of history's great wrongs. Not unreasonable, is it? Well, she was flummoxed. She could only agree.

I think she's got her knickers in a twist recently because of the convoluted story arc she's muddled up in. Feeling a bit mithered as a result. Poor girl can't tell if she's coming or going – or already been.

Upshot is, we go back in time to assassinate Hitler.

Except we don't.

It's Blakey off 'On the Buses.'

We get as far as his office in the depot and we've got him where we want him and then she starts with her transtemporal existential angst again.

How is this affecting her continuity? Is she being consistent? Am I sure that this is Canon?

Does her Backstory look big in this?

Even Blakey off 'On the Buses' looked embarrassed by now, so we shoved him in a cupboard.

So. It was at this point I decided I had had enough.

From my little bag I produced the Time Scrunchy.
And promptly disappeared.
Love,

Panda xx

Dear Panda,

YES! You can catch up with me HERE!

Tune your Time Scrunchy into my cosmic wavelength, love!

I'll stay here and wait.

I'm in the village of Hobbes End and it's May Day 1972. The sun is shining and all the villagers are out dancing around the Maypole.

We're at the end of another thrilling adventure. All my friends from the Ministry of Alien and Other Ontological Wonders are here. Jenny the ex-traffic warden, Barbra the Vending Machine and even that stiff Mida Slike. We've just had a tremendous success putting paid to a coven of wicked witches dabbling with dark forces and calling up the devil!

Now we're going to throw a party. For ridding the world of evil, and also because (it turns out) it's my fifteenth anniversary in print! (Fancy that!) I've invited all kinds of folk to May Day 1972 for a proper old knees up – Tom, Mr Darcy, Heathcliff, Noel Coward, Marlene Dietrich, those blonde alien boys with the blue eyeshadow, Dusty Springfield, the girl from 'Upstairs Downstairs', Robin of Sherwood, Zenith the Albino, Catweazle and his giant green ball bag, the Parisian Countess, Blakey from 'On the Buses', Cagney and Lacey, the giant head of Mr Derek from the Year 5 Billion, several sympathetic Synthethic Men, the Celestial Puppet Master, Fox and Magda Soames, Kristoff Alucard, Professor Challenger and Mrs Hudson, Doctor Van Helsing, the King of Spin-Off Fiction, Vince Cosmos, Poppy Munday, Mrs Wibbsey, The Organ Thief, his hunchbacked boyfriend, Pan's People, TS Eliot, Ngaio Marsh and her giant wasp, Peter Cushing, Brenda and Effie, Samantha the Gestalt Entity, PAND-R, Marco Polo, Mrs Claus and all her elves, and someone who looks a lot like Nerys Hughes.

Will you, won't you, will you join our dance?

Love,

Iris xxx

My Dear Iris,

Why yes, of course!

I shall get my little skates on!

I'll be with you, right there, before you can even say 'Putney Common'.

All love,

Panda xx

Dear Panda,

HURRAY FOR US!

Iris

THE END